Ed 15

SO-AVS-515

DISCARDED

A Follett Beginning-To-Read Book

RIDE, WILLY, RIDE!

Illustrated by
John Mardon

Ride, Willy, Ride!

Carl Memling

FOLLETT PUBLISHING COMPANY
CHICAGO   NEW YORK

Library of Congress Catalog Card Number: 78-85950

ISBN 0 695-80087-6 trade binding
ISBN 0 695-40087-8 titan binding

First Printing E

There was once a rancher and his wife. They
lived in a little old ranch house in the middle
of a wide prairie in the old Wild West.

They had a boy named Willy, and they were
very proud of him.

One day Willy's mother saw a band
of outlaws far, far out on the prairie.

She called to her husband. He called to
Willy. Willy came running.

Willy's father said, "Willy, saddle your horse
and run for help. Outlaws are coming. We'll stay
here and try to hold them off till you get back.
So ride for help, Willy, and come back in time.
Ride, Willy, ride!"

Willy ran and saddled his horse and rode away as fast as he could.

His mother and father called after him, "Ride, Willy, ride!"

Soon Willy came to the band of outlaws.

"Stop!" they shouted.

But Willy did not stop.

The fastest outlaw went chasing after
Willy. He rode as fast as he could.
But he could not catch Willy.

Willy rode on till he met two big growling bears.

He called to them, "I am Willy of the little old ranch. I rode faster than the outlaws' fastest man. And I can go faster than you, I can!"

The two big bears gave two big growls,
"GRRRRR! GRRRRR!"
 And they ran after Willy.
 The two big bears ran as fast as they could.
 But they could not catch Willy.

Willy rode on and on, faster and faster!
He rode till he met three shaggy buffaloes.

He called to them, "I am Willy of the little
old ranch. I rode faster than the outlaws'
fastest man, faster than two big growling bears.
And I can go faster than you, I can!"

The buffaloes lowered their heads. They stamped and they bellowed.

Then they ran after Willy.

The three shaggy buffaloes ran as fast as they could.

But they could not catch Willy.

Willy rode on and on till he met four
mountain lions.

Willy called out to them, "I am Willy of
the little old ranch. I rode faster than
the outlaws' fastest man, faster than two
big growling bears and three shaggy buffaloes.
And I can go faster than you, I can!"

The four mountain lions roared at Willy.
Then they ran after him. They ran as fast as
they could.

But they could not catch Willy.

Willy rode on and on till at last he came to some cowboys camping.

He stopped his horse, and he called to them, "I am Willy of the little old ranch. Outlaws have come to our ranch. My mother and father are holding them off. But I must bring help as soon as I can."

"I rode faster than the outlaws' fastest man,
faster than two big growling bears and three
shaggy buffaloes and four roaring mountain lions.
Please cowboys, help me—if you can."

"We'll do what we can. Turn right around, Willy, ride back to the ranch. We will ride after you."

So Willy turned around.

He rode and he rode as fast as he could.

The cowboys rode after him, shouting,

"Ride, Willy, ride."

Soon Willy called back, "Only *three* miles to go!"

Next, he called, "Only *two* miles to go!
Then, he called, "Only *one* mile to go!"

At last Willy shouted, "WE'RE HERE!"
Willy and the cowboys arrived just in time!
The outlaws were near the ranch house!

The cowboys chased the outlaws away and saved the rancher and his wife.

No wonder the rancher and his wife were so proud of their son Willy!

RIDE, WILLY, RIDE!

Reading Level: Level Three. *Ride, Willy, Ride!* has a total vocabulary of 144 words. It has been tested in third grade classes, where it was read with ease.

Uses of this Book: Reading for fun. When outlaws come to the old ranch house, brave young Willy makes an adventurous ride for help.

Word List

All of the 144 words used in *Ride, Willy, Ride!* are listed. Regular possessives and contractions (-'s, -n't, -'ll, -'m) and regular verb forms (-s, -ed, -ing) of words already on the list are not listed separately, but the endings are given in parentheses after the word.

5 there	of	saw
was	wide	band
once	prairie	outlaw(s)(s')
a	wild	far
ranch(er)	west	out
and	had	on
his	boy	she
wife	named	called
they	Willy('s)	to
lived	were	her
in	very	husband
little	proud	he
old	him	came
house	6 one	run(ning)
the	day	7 father
middle	mother	said

saddle(d)
your
horse
for
help
are
coming
we'll
stay
here
try
hold(ing)
them
off
till
you
get
back
so
ride
come
time
8 ran
rode
away
as
fast(er)(est)
could
after
10 soon
stop(ped)
shouted

but
did
not
11 went
chasing
catch
12 met
two
big
growling
bears
I
am
than
man
can
go
15 gave
growls
grrrrr
16 three
shaggy
buffaloes
19 lowered
their
heads
stamped
bellowed
then
20 four
mountain
lions

21 roared
at
22 last
some
cowboys
camping
have
our
must
bring
23 roaring
please
me
if
24 do
what
turn(ed)
right
around
25 shouting
26 only
mile(s)
next
we're
arrived
just
near
28 chased
saved
29 no
wonder
son

31

The Follett BEGINNING-TO-READ Books

Purpose of the Beginning-to-Read Books: To provide easy-to-read materials that will appeal to the interests of primary children. Careful attention is given to vocabulary load and sentence length, but the first criterion is interest to children.

Reading Levels: These books are written at three reading levels, indicated by one, two, or three dots beneath the *Beginning-to-Read* symbol on the back cover. *Level One* books can be read by first grade children in the last half of the school year. As children increase their reading ability they will be able to enjoy *Level Two* books. And as they grow further in their reading ability they will progress to *Level Three* books. Some first grade children will read *Level Two* and *Level Three* books. Many third graders, and even some fourth graders, will read and enjoy *Level One* and *Level Two* books, as well as *Level Three* books. The range of interest of *Beginning-to-Read* books stretches far beyond their reading level.

Use of the Beginning-to-Read Books: Because of their high interest and readability, these books are ideal for independent reading by primary children—at school, in the library, and at home. The books may also be incorporated into the basic reading program to develop children's interests, expand their vocabularies, and improve word-attack skills. It has been suggested that they might serve as the foundation for a skillfully directed reading program. Many *Beginning-to-Read* books correlate with the social studies, science, and other subject fields. All will help children grow in the language arts. Children will read the *Beginning-to-Read* books with confidence, with success, and with real enjoyment.